OLD SOULS

AND THE

GRAMMAR

OF

THEIR WANDERINGS

OLD SOULS AND THE GRAMMAR OF THEIR WANDERINGS
Copyright © 2013 Berrien C. Henderson
All Rights Reserved Worldwide
Papaveria Press
France

ISBN 978 1 907881 23 7

Printed in Great Britain

www.papaveria.com

Old Souls
and the
Grammar
of
Their Wanderings

Berrien C. Henderson

TABLE OF CONTENTS

DEDICATION

FOR BECKY — HER LOVE, HER FRIENDSHIP, HER
SUPPORT.

AND HEATH AND ABBY — HOW YOU TEACH ME EACH DAY
AND INSPIRE ME.

FOREWORD

I LIKE QUILTS, ESPECIALLY OLD SCHOOL PATCHWORKS— granny quilts that tell a story spun by the gnarled, facile hands that pieced them together from saved scraps because each piece spoke or murmured or whispered or reminded.

Myths and legends exert their relevance across historical and cultural boundaries with such common threads that stitch them together yet with the pop and vibrancy and texture of careful additions. For Arthuriana, there are some anonymous Welsh poets. Then came Chretien de Troyes. Didot. Robert de Boron. Geoffrey of Monmouth. An imprisoned, indebted soldier named Malory. A grieving laureate in Tennyson. As distinctly British as the Arthurian legends appear, they're nothing more than echoes sounding across centuries and still quite happily and heroically bouncing around, reverberating through popular culture. E.B. White for starters. On this side of the pond, even Steinbeck had a go at the noble knights. The Monty Python guys. Or those merry folks at Marvel Comics. Disney. The BBC and SyFy. And I'd be sorely remiss not to include Stephen King's *Dark Tower* series in this little list of antecedents.

But let me go back to one particular source for a moment—two, actually. Poor old de Troyes, for whatever reason, falls into that auspicious department of Writers

Who Never Finished What They Started, what with the narrative *interruptus* of *Perceval*, and leave it to scholars to be original enough to call the First and Second Continuations as much, but somebody (or a couple of somebodies) wasted little time getting the characters back on their respective, legendary paths. So, the rest of the Arthurian patchworkers followed suit.

All I ever wanted to do was give some of the characters amnesia (or a literary hangover) and work them into the Deep South. After all, there's plenty of Celtic influence here 'bouts to inform such a retelling, but what helped keep me on track was concern. It's a fine line to walk and not spin out those folks as the love children of Jeff Foxworthy and Malory—or some such as a friend of mine cautioned me at the outset. Here's hoping the advice and the results paid off.

The pair of stories in this tiny collection are only a couple of tales fitting into what I've come to call the Fogle County stories. It's been my good fortune to have several folks in my corner and helping me get them out there—not least in Erzebet YellowBoy. I'm indebted to her for her guidance and not a bit of nudging.

I'm furthermore grateful you've stopped to sit a spell and read about some old familiar friends.

Oh, don't forget to snuggle up under the quilt.
And enjoy.

—BCH

OLD LANGUAGE

1

The fence had died,
Perishing by solemn degrees,
Choked to silence by bullis vines
Lurking on the ground
And slithering like fertility symbols
Through trees that suffered
Their subtle visitations.
I crossed forgotten boundaries
As the wind explored
The hairs of my arms.
The open sky and sweet-crisp odor
Of new green greet me—
A prodigal edging home.
A sigh from the land,
Thinking itself hidden in time
And its paths unstuck,
Napping in shadows
Between heartbeats and breaths.

2

A two-path road bumped and curled
Around a field forgetful of its own history,
An amnesiac struggling to move on.
The old crops are gone,
But the wind and birds had brought pine and plum.
The grass, broomsage — tall, fat, frayed-end things
Nodding like a congregation of wizened Pentecostals.
God cast an invisible stone
Into this pond of grass.
Sine waves danced across the stalks.

3

A red-tailed hawk gyred above a mouse.
I watched this documentary full of parable—
It's a hungry evening
After the bones of the wild
Rolled up nothing.
The far hollow called the hawk—
An old oak a threshold
At a crenellation of treeline
Fronting the south bank of a pond
That warded turtles, fish, and snakes—
A veritable Hecate's stew.
Into the hollow he flew,
And my eyes seized his flight,
A vanishing of wings, a soft glide.
Godspeed.

4

Gone and gone and far,
I imagined a thread attached to the hawk
And leading me beyond the cusp
Of green and shadow.
I'm guilty of pagan urges,
Thoughts of researching mistletoe and mandrake,
Spinning out phonemes for gods of hemlock
And the binding of spirits.
I wandered in a hush — no breeze and nothing
But the hawk, the mouse, and me,
Familiars each in each,
Something past and faraway in that field,
A whispering of earth, a slow shifting.
I moved, though the feet be rooted in dirt,
Became my own language,
And in a moment, old.

A MATTER OF ANACHRONISMS, ARCHETYPAL YET CURIOUS IN THEIR IMPLICATIONS

PRELUDE

HERE LIES SNYTACTIC MYSTERY FROM STRANGE AND ALIEN tongues, unstuck and bound to the land where "Once upon a time" wedges itself in the treated-pine cracks in the doorstep of a drunkard's single-wide trailer, and holy blood and holy roods warp to nothing more than cheap wine and scarecrow staves out of some dead land.

Write it on your heart.

Mark it ye.

Listen.

Come...

1
WHEREIN A GAELIC AMNESIAC BECOMES A BY-WORD UNTO HIMSELF

IT IS ALWAYS TWILIGHT IN MY DREAMS. LIGHT HAUNTS AND MOCKS itself. Razors cut the night—meteors from out of Perseus strake ghost-ice passages through the void. And sometimes, despite the twilight, I believe I am an amnesiac near-god. I need to get back my gun soon. Soon. Soon.

He had dozed again, thankfully again, in the recliner. Then his head wanted to implode.

Art had been drunk last night and had been reading Joyce's *Ulysses* and, for a time, forgotten himself. Not quite like forgetting himself just drinking—again, somewhere in the gray that was last night—but close. He had to over the hangover first, which was why he'd been nursing it for a couple hours since sunrise over a potent concoction of 32 oz. of Gatorade along with three ibuprofen, two naproxen sodium tabs, and a double-shot of Goody's headache powders. And coffee. Lots of it. So long as his liver didn't turn toxic, it might be a decent day.

He had much to consider going into the end of the week.

To wit: He reached over and found the button on the answering machine and hit PLAY.

Click. Buzz-whine.

"Hey, Art. It's Earl Martin. Other than some technicalities, we're set for the your getting the land.

All a frivolous, last-ditch litiginous effort on your half-brother's part as I'd said before. You're looking at the usual paperwork--copies and such. Just come by the office, say, Friday of this week so that we can go over final costs, which we'd discussed previously. See you soon."

Kla-tunk. Reee-beep.

So, all Art needed was a several hundred dollars to settle up with Mr. Martin.

Then there was the matter of settling up with Mr. Stone at the pawn shop—the real trick, now, wasn't it? Getting the family gun back out of hock. He could care less about the inheritance, after two years, finally going through, just glad it was all over. Or he could keep lying to himself.

He picked up *Ulysses* off the end table and pulled out the thin bookmark. A worn piece of paper. One of two, actually, because all Mr. Martin had needed was one copy—good enough.

He read a note that was actually almost three years old:

"Art, This is my artifact to you—a spot of land, a parcel of apology. What would grow here rests within you. My gift, then: 300 acres for 1 (one) dollar and love and affection."

[signed] Luther Penderton

He folded the note and stuck it back in the book. His vision blurred, and some invisible vise-grip found his skull.

It would be a long day.

And he still had painting to do over at Mrs. Brown's, just some touch-up painting under the eaves of the roof, then caulking sometime tomorrow.

He took a long draw on the Gatorade jug and thought about the work to do. And hoped the galley proofs of his chapbook would be in the mail; that would be nice. Some simple concession of the USPS shipping schedule. As much a concession as lucking into the presence of one C.V. Deal, sometime friend, ofttime borrower of every other tool Art owned, which wasn't saying much.

Art kept hydrating. The day was yet young.

2
ONWARD THE DAY – GAS DRIVE-OFF – C.V. – WOUNDED MAN – QUESTING BEAST

ONCE HE MADE IT TO THE SURE EXPRESS ON HIS WAY INTO Urville, the county seat of Fogle, Art appreciated the bit of cool breeze knocking around up under the shaded gas pump island as he struggled through the sweeping gray claw-thing in his head. It would be a couple hours before he could try shutting his liver down again with over-the-counter medicine. He watched the dollars and cents and tenths of a gallon *cla-tick*, *cla-tick*, *cla-tick* away and let his thoughts get trapped somewhere between paying what he owed Mr. Martin for legal fees and services rendered on the inheritance settlement, paying Mr. Stone for the double-barreled shotgun in pawn, and, hellfire and damnation, at least sixty dollars for gas that some suits had been claiming record quarterly profits on for three years and still not manage to find a way to eek out under three dollars a gallon. And C.V. He needed his tools back from C.V., damn his time.

A vehicle, loud with its only half-functioning exhaust, throated to a stop, and the door creaked open and rattle-clanged shut.

Hanging up the gas nozzle, reaching into the truck's cab to get the 32 oz. Sure Express franchise's Sure 'nough Big Mug (tm) – free refills, by God – Art went in to pay for the gas. He had to walk by the other gas-tank island, but the last thing he needed was to walk past that other truck.

"Heard Wayne's back in town," came a voice at the other pump.

Art took a few more steps.

"Listen, Art. Ya got Pa's land and the trailer and all the farm equipment."

Art turned to the man with greasy black hair and squinted, near-sighted eyes. He took a deep breath. "Hey, Morris. You don't have to remind me of the proceedings. It's been a month since—"

"It's been two and a half years, Art," said Morris. He took a step forward, and Art dearly wanted to beat the living shit out of his half-brother.

Another deep breath. "Two and a half years, then. Standing here jawin' 'bout it ain't gonna change a thing," he said. He watched Morris pretend that pumping his gas was more important.

"Bygones," said Morris.

"I reckon," said Art. He entered the store.

Mug in hand, he put four packs of artificial sweetner in it along with some hazlenut creamer. If nothing else, the mug was a constant companion and a comforter. A man ought to have a good coffee mug despite the quality of the coffee he might put in it.

"Howdy, Art," said Dawn the clerk.

He grabbed two packs of beef jerky. "Yo."

The guttural exhalations of Morris's truck reached into the store.

"You want me to ring up something extra?"

"Meaning what, Dawn?"

"Morris just pulled off without paying," she said. She also couldn't attest to the colorful euphony of Art's cursing under his breath.

He set the mug on the counter and the beef jerky, too. He thumbed out bills for his fuel and fare, his fingertips hesitating.

"Want I call Craig?" she said, referring to Urville's deputy.

"No, I'll pay for it," said Art. He added more money, stuck the jerky in his back pocket, and nodded to Dawn.

"You're a good man, Art," said Dawn as he pushed open the door.

He gave a her a sidelong look and said, "Just a rumor I started a few years ago."

Dawn's chuckling followed him out and hung thick in his hungover head even as he drove out 203 to Ritch Road on his way to work on the widow Perkins's pump. She'd called yesterday evening right before his little bender, and he wouldn't tell her how lucky she was that he'd written it down before the 100 proof party had started to flow in ye olde Penderton veins.

Easing off onto a dirt road, Art slowed as he saw someone walking up ahead. He rolled down his window.

"Hey, C.V."

The blond man stopped and turned as Art braked and put the Ford in park. "Good morning, Art. Man, you look like you've been rode hard and put up wet."

Art held up the Sure 'nough Big Mug. "Got just the elixir for the job, though. Speaking of. I got to go see widow Perkins about a water pump problem. How 'bout you come along, keep me company."

"Mind taking me to see Old Man Fisher after a while?" said C.V. He was already getting in the truck.

"Sure. How's he doing?"

"Incorrigible and stubborn."

"Happens sometimes," said Art, putting the truck in

gear and easing on down the road. "By the way, you still got my tools?"

"Not on me," said C.V. with a grin.

"Smartass, I know that," said Art. He drank deeply of the coffee and thanked the Lord for such things as Gatorade, OTC pain relief, and caffeine. "So, help me a little on the water pump, and I won't hassle you anymore today about those tools I loaned you. And I got to call James later about some pecan tree saplings I'm gonna plant this Saturday. You might could come by and help with that, too, you take the notion."

"Deal."

They bumped and shimmied along the dirt road.

That afternoon Art and C.V. found themselves knocking on a screen door and peering in.

"Come on in!" said Old Man Fisher.

The screen door *eeee-riii-ed* its rodent sound on ancient hinges. In a gold slipcovered recliner sat Old Man Fisher. He had just a pudge for a belly and a bald pate—a friar's mark, Art thought. The past year's convalescence hadn't helped an otherwise active man and sometimes farmer and driver of tractors for other local farmers who might need his help and pay him in gas or beer or barbecue betimes. The pink stump of shin just below the right knee was an eye-magnet, and Fisher, cognizant of this, pulled a purple woolen fleece over his legs.

"Boys raised in a barn or what? Take a seat," he said and motioned to slipcovered chairs flanking a ratty loveseat.

"Hey, Fisher," said C.V.

A nod. "C.V. Art, been a while. You through with your schooling off to Valdosta way?"

"Yes, sir. Been piddling with odd jobs until something comes open in the school system."

"State job with good benefits. If you was to quit, have to get a real job," said Fisher.

They all laughed.

Old Man Fisher's eyes glittered for a moment, the way Art remembered them from his own childhood and from when the man drove a school bus part-time, too. Nobody ever gave him guff, and if they had, well, Fisher had an easy way yet stern tongue that managed to remind most kids into a contrite spot where one might think of a grandfather pulling out a pocketknife and cutting a switch for a swift swish or two to the posterior.

"You doing all right otherwise?" said Fisher after a moment's silence. Which was to say: "Sorry your daddy saved some folks' lives down to Dixon's Country Store during a robbery two years gone. He was a good man, your daddy."

Art shoved down the hurt and blackness long enough to say, "Gettin' good at gettin' by."

"'bout all you can do. How 'bout your the land and legal issues?"

It wasn't a smile that creased Art's face. Nevertheless: "Just glad I'm shed of it."

"Lawyers," grumbled Fisher.

"Well, 'cept Mr. Martin," said Art.

"Coulda done worse."

"That might've cost more."

Fisher laughed. The stump moved under the blanket as if it wanted to peek out. "Ain't that how it goes? Anyhow, what can I do for you boys?"

C.V. said, "Just dropped by to see if you need us to run any errands."

"Meh. Maybe take some money to that girl down to the Satilla River Landing down Voight Bridge way. Brought me some preserves the other day. Could use the money, I suppose."

He grabbed a crutch and *ooffed* up and hop-crutched into the next room. At the countertop in the kitchen, he took some money out of a billfold and put money in an envelope and wrote something on the envelope.

"Takin' your insulin like you 'pose to?" said C.V.

"Since when do I need you to nanny me?" said Old Man Fisher.

Art snorted. "Both of you sound like a pair of crows."

"You and your friend'd shit, too, you eat regular," said Fisher.

C.V. said, "No disrespect, but look what gettin' a frog gig stuck in your calf earned you."

Fisher fiddled with putting the money in the envelope. He gave a wry smile. "Ain't so much to look at. You know, I can still feel the damned thing. Helluva note when you lose a limb, and it hurts where it *used* to be." He handed the envelope to C.V. "Tell ol' girl the strawberry preserves are still delicious but pro'ly not for long."

"Will do."

C.V. and Art watched Old Man Fisher take some Vicodin.

"Yeah, still hurts," he said.

So, C.V. had impressed the anecdote upon Art. To wit, the runaway lived at the old Gill house out Voight

Bridge way near the Little Satilla Landing. She was living in thrall to a ten-foot-long albino rattlesnake that hypnotized her into taking care of it under the crawlspace of the house. "She's been calling it a Questing Beast," said C.V.

The name unhinged something anchored deep in synaptic wrinkles as Art said, "Take me there." He thought, *There's folk in the mountains who would do some sure-enough dancing in the Spirit over one like that.*

Art's Ford F250 jiggled and creaked down the washboard dirt road. He ran through a stop sign and eased onto Voight Bridge Road.

"Just how do you come by this compelling story?" said Art. The river was low enough you could walk it from the bridge a half mile to the landing; he had fond memories of doing just that in junior high.

C.V. said, "Ol' Phillip told me."

"Phillip says a lot," said Art, underwhelmed. "You know I'm only going out here because Old Man Fisher asked us to shuttle money for the jam she'd made him."

"Uh-huh," said C.V. "Got anything better to do yourself?"

"Beside ferretting out some bit of local folklore about ophidian mesmerists and strange young women?" Art turned.

"You ain't got to use them big words," said C.V. "And like dealing with Eva's any different? Or Vera?"

"That is different."

"Uh-huh."

The dirt road's tongue lolled amid acres of planted pines—all dry, wasted after a few years of drought. They came to the old Gill house. So near the river, the house stood on cinder block columns; the place stood a good four feet off the ground. Cream-colored paint peeled off the warped wood siding. It had, of recent years, been an accepted (though frowned upon) haven for squatters, this girl-woman Morgan one of them. She was working outside. She had black hair and a cream face and jade eyes like the sun on spring leaves in April after a rain. She wasn't unkempt—just as kempt as a person could be given the situation. And it was understandable the way she looked at these two men getting out of the pickup. Deliberate, guarded mistrust.

Art offered a disarming smile and waved. "Afternoon. Old Man Fisher says you brought him some strawberry preserves," he said.

"Yeah, and?" She folded her arms. How many times had she been approached by men? What had she learned on whatever roads that had brought her here? Art wondered and was not surprised nor put-off.

"Well, he sent us to say thank you." He held up the envelope so she could read the flap. "Said he owed you ten bucks for the two jars' worth."

She stood there, arms still folded, then accepted the envelope. "Appreciate it."

"He does, too."

She glanced at C.V. "So, you need anything, or was last week good enough?" she said.

C.V. tapped out a cigarette and flicked out his Zippo. "Naw. I'm good, probably 'til next week, lessen you want to come to Art's party tomorrow night."

"Let me check my schedule and get back with you," she said with a glittering laugh that surprised the both of them.

Then behind her back at the house came the most regional and peculiar of warnings from a brace of rattles. Morgan's eyes widened; Art felt an icepick jam itself in his psyche.

Cut the small talk and innuendo. Come see why you rode out here.

In a trice Morgan's eyes had glazed over, and her full lips opened—any former sensuality gone with a slack jaw Art guesstimated dialed her back about thirty to forty IQ points.

Don't mind her. Now, you. You're a treat.

The words undulated through his head, and he felt compelled to follow Morgan, who moved like an automaton. C.V. was now sitting on the open tailgate and oblivious to the goings on while he continued his smoke.

That'sssss it.

Art and Morgan stooped to duck-crawl under the house. Enough light fell so they could see where stray dogs had once dug pits in which to flop and slumber, but no more. Gaping mouth-holes where woods rats had burrowed peppered other spots. In the cool dark under the exposed floor joists hung any number of spiderwebs. All a haunt for things stray and feral and opportunistic.

Staring at them, its head the size of a man's fist, its body thigh-thick and ten feet long, waited the rattlesnake. C.V.'s fable. Phillip's folktale.

The head lifted off the ground and gauged them with ever-flared pits. The bifurcated tongue tasted the air; Art knew it tasted them and shuddered.

The rattlesnake was albino.

Reverently, Morgan took something out of her pocket. She mumbled silently—and Art imagined a mute's liturgy—while unwrapping a piece of burlap sack. She shoved the flaccid offering, nudged it, so that the snake might accept it. Art's nostrils quivered when he detected some gamey odor.

The serpent eased to the dead rat, then looked up at Art.

It's so much easier this way. And I am old.

"How old?" said Art. His own voice sounded far away. He glanced at Morgan, whose face was slack.

Then came the dried-beans-in-their-pods noise of the rattles. *I weigh over one hundred pounds. Am albino, as you clearly see. Can mesmerize and sling glamour with the best of them. In fact, you and your friend will barely remember this encounter—just your bringing the Wounded Man's money to this minx who so readily feeds me rats and the occasional feline. Oh, and the best strawberry preserves in three counties.*

The snake seemed to smile, and Art chuckled nervously.

I will give birth soon. My own young will kill and eat me.

"Didn't know rattlesnake young did that," said Art.

They don't because they aren't. It stretched its head, brushing the floor joists. *Just the best avatar I could assume under the circumstances. If you somehow find yourself dreaming of this moment, this conversation, might I suggest taking a stiff drink. You do drink, don't you?*

"I quit last night," said Art, "but resuming tonight won't be a problem."

A prolonged hiss. *Poison of choice?*

"Southern Comfort."

Capital. Now, go.

Art backed out of there as his clarity returned by degrees. He dusted himself off and hurried to the truck. Morgan stayed behind and sang softly—some children's song, some charm, something that had lost all puissance long, long ago.

"Come on, C.V."

"Well?"

"What?"

"The rattler? See it?"

"Ain't no rattler," said Art, cranking the truck. "Just some more of Phillip's bullshit."

C.V. took one last draw from his cigarette and thumped it to the dirt and ground it under his heel as he got in the truck. The door squeaked in protest, the window glass rattling upon closing. "Knew it. At least the girl's easy on the eyes. Think she'll show to the party?"

Art drove back out in silence after he shrugged.

3
EX CALCE LIBERATUS

IF HE HAD CARED TO READ INSTEAD OF DRINKING, HE MIGHT have felt better. But he had put in close to an honest day's work (by the end of the day) and could've used some company (that's what tomorrow night was for, wasn't it?).

Still, it was careless of him to get drunk to the point he turned frustrated and violent. Who was there to vent upon? Just himself.

You got the land, after all that fighting. The farm's yours, he thought in a short-lived moment of clarity. Maybe Morris was right.

A swig for estranged half-brothers.

Dead broke and damned can't manage, college boy.

A swig for callous pawn brokers.

The Southern Comfort was 100 proof velvet on his tongue and throat. He studied the bottle and its sloshing vitality. He turned his attention to the double-barreled shotgun—well, the barrels themselves since that sonuvabitch Stone wouldn't let Art have it back entire. It had been almost three weeks since he'd tried talking the man into letting him get the whole gun out of hock. He'd given Stone six hundred dollars of what he owed, and Stone had as much laughed in his face.

"Partial payment, partial gun."

"My ass."

Art set the bottle down and wavered upon standing up. He followed a snaky invisible line to the propped up barrels. He grabbed them and stared with bleary eyes at the vine motif engraved along the blued steel. The face and beard, imbued with leaves, of a man appeared in the vines. "Green Man," he slurred aloud, surprising himself as memories of his Medieval English Literature (*literachoor* as he sometimes lapsed in the argot of they of the dusty dirt roads and rusted-out vehicles hiding in the grown-over backyards would ascribe). The gun—whole—was three generations old. It had been his since he was fourteen.

He walked out on his back porch and looked out over the pond. The sunset had inverted itself into the watery irreality. Bream popped the surface like creatures pressing the mystic cellophane threshold between a lost Gaelic world. He walked off the porch and stumbled to the shore and frightened a bullfrog in his drunken advance. With a trifecta of malice aforethought, alcoholic lunacy, and plain old self-loathing, Art threw the gun barrels in the water and watched the ripples run concentric races toward the far shore.

He staggered back to his trailer, then staggered back to the pond with his whiskey sidekick in tow. Plopping on the bank, he saw the pond absorb the sunset and evening's ink and compose, as usual, his best poetry while drunk. Eva, the witch living on the other end of the pond, waved to him from the far shore. He could hear her singing as she turned to go back into her tiny shotgun-shack farmhouse. Then he lay back, looked up at some first magnitude stars for all of two minutes, and passed out.

A small wake split the water as something moved just beneath the surface to come onto the bank near

Art. A slender, scaly form flopped onto the ground and with its ovoid head and flared gills looked around until it saw him. Saw him with its thoroughly human eyes. Mist condensed around it as it bucked and melted and shifted into human form, and there stood the witch Eva, dripping pond water and touched here and there with algae on her twenty-year-old body that was one hundred fifty years old. Water pearled on her breasts and shone in the starlight at the mystery of her hips. Her hair was the night. She leaned over Art and whispered archaic terms he read as footnotes in college. After she turned to slip back into the pond, Art stumbled back into his trailer.

The pond accepted Eva wholly as stars played in the ripples.

4
BECAUSE TAKING ONE'S INHERITANCE FOR GRANTED IS OFTEN A BIBLICAL AND FABULISTIC INEVITABILITY

FOR ART THE NEXT MORNING TURNED HIM TOWARD TWO letters of equal importance though differing subject matter. One came with the discovery of the barrels he'd tossed the night before into the pond. Now they lay on the back porch and covered in a sheet like a shroud — grave-clothes for a thing redeemed. On top of the wrapped barrels was a note:

> Art,
> You shouldn't be so quick, even in drunkenness, to throw away your heritage. So, I made sure to clean up your mess of it, get all the mud and muck and fish-shit off the steel and out the barrels and lightly oil it. Here it is along with some free advice.
> It is not what a gun has done, but rather what is has come to mean in the symbology of your family's history. I remember the squirrels you shot with it. Do you? I'm sure, too, it has gathered dust in a corner, most notably during your years of college when academics and other things besides home took precedent in your life. Very well. But to whore it to a place with 300% interest (at least!) just to redeem it and hurl it into the

pond?!? Who in the hells do you think you
are? You have done no less than forgotten
who you are and where you've come from.

[signed] Nyna Faye Evangeline

To take his mind off further self-loathing and
thoughts of Eva's tending to her own business on her
own damned side of the pond, he went to the small
breakfast table where he'd placed the day's mail. A
smattering of junk mail and notices fanned out on the
grimy tabletop along with a 9" x 12" envelope. *Yes, it finally
came*, he thought, quickly tearing into the package.

4A
[CAMERA-READY PAGE FROM *A MISCELLANY OF DIRT ROADS*]

ART,

Here are those proof pages for the chapbook. Have a look and make any notations you see fit. If it finds you in good order, maybe this will to: I nixed the original idea of running 150 copies and am willing to boost it to 300 instead and will throw in a few postcard promos and a sheaf of broadsides. Just something to think about.

[signed] Slade St. John
Editor
Horn's Call Press

Art flipped through the galley proofs and paused to read.

flocks of crows burst
like India ink splatters
Rorshach in the sky

mist on broken earth
a gathering of soft hands
kneading ancient flesh

pond stumps pierce water
dawn mist skirts glass surface
clouds amid mountaintops

sermons find occasion
between crickets' chirping

Yes. Three hundred copies sounded nice, he thought.

5
THE TABLE ROUND, ITS SIEGE PARLOUS, AND THE UNRAVELING OF KINSHIPS

ALMOST EVERYONE HAD ARRIVED FOR ART'S SHINDIG.

Art sat on the overturned five-gallon bucket. It had been—what? months?—since he'd had friends over. The old pack. The comitatus. Back for some *esprit de corps*.

C.V. kept the fire stoked. Lance and Morris bickered over the virtues of Fords and Chevrolets and immigration and gas prices. Vera had come by, fashionably late, to play madame socialite and flittered like the sparking, soon-flashed-out sparks tumbling in the fire's convections. She stayed near Lance.

In the night it was easy for them to come unstuck, especially Art, especially amid the orange arcana of flames and the inky press of night. Somewhere on the far side of the pond, the witch Eva sang, and they listened to her alien tongues as Art got up and went inside, returning with a case of beer which he plunked on the old industrial sized utility spool now serving as a table.

"What y'all waiting for?" said Art, and the beer went fast. By the time he'd gotten three in himself, he'd stopped mingling and took a moment to compose the haiku that had been tumbling through his head all day.

> nighttime jets flashing
> along a hedgerow of clouds
> fireflies at Mach two

"Can't you leave off that fuckin' shit?" said Morris.

"Says the troglodyte," said Art, getting another beer.

"Anything else snobby you got to say? You got a book coming out. Won our daddy's land." Morris stood and dusted off his pants from the hay bale.

Lance stepped in as he always had. "Morris, ain't the time nor the place. High school's been over for five years now."

"Ain't never been time nor place, Lance, so don't touch me, goddammit," hissed Morris, and Lance saw in the other's eyes that there would be absolutely no honor, no rationale, no peace even for a few hours this night.

"Knew I shouldn't've invited you," said Art, holding off opening the beer as Morris swaggered over.

"You'd've been informed not to have invited a couple folks," said Morris, his eyes darting to Vera and Lance. "Too damned nai—"

And Art popped him in the head with the unopened beer; Morris crumpled and got shakily to his knees. Red ire flashed across his bleary eyes. The bottom of the beer can had imprinted on his forehead; the red weal inscribed thereon spoke wrath.

"One more word, and I will stomp a mudhole in your ass and walk the fucker dry." Art stood over Morris, and a wave of deja vu swelled over him the way it had yesterday at the pond. Old hatred—eld bitterness—welled in his eyes. If only there had been a snake insinuating itself in the yard between them, how apropos? From across the pond the witch's song paused in some tenuous caesura. Art said, "Pick yourself up and go. Or stay down."

As Morris wrenched himself up to try lunging for Art, who just stood there in dread calm, Lance and Wayne each found one of Morris's arms.

"Not so fast, big un," said Lance.

"Let go," growled Morris.

"And let him prove he's not so drunk now as you? Maybe some other time," said Wayne. "Good seein' you, Art."

"Wish it had been longer," said Art.

"I won't forget this," said Morris as the other two carted him off to Lance's truck.

"Promises, promises," said Art.

So, the fire died by degrees with the sullen turn of events, but C.V. hung around and kicked his feet up on the utility-spool table. He waved bye to them.

"Just like Morris to go and kill the whole mood," said C.V. He craned his neck to look at Art. "Toldja."

"Good night, C.V." Art had a thousand things to say. One of them was that C.V. was right. Just not right now.

"Later, tater." C.V. stood and flickered an index finger wave. He walked into the night, which folded him into it itself. "Well enough. Even ol' girl never showed."

A piece of wood popped in the fire.

"Art."

Vera stood at the front stoop of the trailer.

"Thanks for coming," he said as he negotiated the steps. That they were already wobbly, and so were his alchohol-infused legs didn't help. He grabbed the doorknob.

Vera folded her arms. "My ride left."

"Shame, that." He turned the knob.

"Could you drive me home?"

"Sure, if I weren't halfway drunk," he said with a snort. "You know, Lance ain't seen Wayne in over a year. Some catching up to do. You know how Lance gets."

Vera just stared at him.

He pulled from his pint of Southern Comfort. "Far be it for me to turn away a damsel in distress." He took another draught.

"Smartass sonuvabitch."

"There's plenty of wood for the fire," said Art, opening the door. "It's 'posed to get cold tonight."

"Couch still warm?"

Art went in and left the trailer door open. In she came, and in the low light of the interior, her face shimmered as Art plopped onto the couch.

"Thought the couch was mine tonight," she said.

"Mine every night," said Art, sighing drunkenly, his eyelids thickening and drooping.

She plied him with charms and spangles and not a little Southern Comfort while her face swam in shadows—first her own, then somehow Eva's, and the strange river-girl Morgan.

"Wha?" he managed as her hands fluttered over his belt buckle and button and zipper.

"Shhhhhhhhh," came a rippling voice, at once in his ear and across the room. "Just taking care of you."

And the shadow of a feminine trinity that wrought glamour and warmth in his veins and against secret places along his skin.

6
EX CALCE LIBERATUS REDUX OR SETTLING UP IS HARD TO DO

THE MORNING CAME AS THICK AND SLUGGISH AS ART'S own waking.

Mr. Stone chomped a half-smoked Swisher Sweet and grinned around it as the brass bell heralded Art's entrance.

Art reached into his pocket and pulled out folded bills. "Mr. Stone." He nodded.

"Afternoon, Art. What can I do you for?"

"Well, since you put it that way. Look. You said I could redeem the gun."

"The gun parts."

"Parts, then, for four hundred bucks." He counted out the twenties and fives he'd gotten for fixing the widow Perkins's pump. The tens for hauling off deadwood for ol' Edsel. The fifty from the caulking job—post-painting—for Mrs. Brown. He pushed the bills across the countertop. "Here."

"Pawn ticket?"

Art could have come across the display case. "You just hold on a damned minute. You're going to hassle me for a receiver and buttstock and the foregrip after I already got the barrels?"

Mr. Stone chewed the Swisher Sweet. Slowly. "I get meth tweaks in here a good bit. Construction workers who pawn their own toolbelts. Fella come in to pawn a gun just yesterday, probably for cash to cover bad checks—had the look about him. All kinds. You, though. You come in with a two thousand dollar custom twelve gauge. Family heirloom. Get a clean thousand for it. Go on a bender for two weeks and come up dry as a bone on what you owed that lawyer Martin"—he raised a hand to stifle Art's interjection—"and you *need* some-damned-body to *not* give you what you *want*. Plus, it's my perogative to hassle as I see fit."

Art blinked. So, he was at a disadvantage in this study of small town mercantilism and market influences. He tapped a fingertip on the money spread out on the countertop. "I've got the money. And gas ain't no cheaper for you than for me."

"Still, I've got the rest of your gun." Mr. Stone took the old blunt out of his mouth and pointed it at Art. "Got what Luther had. Got what your granddaddy Troy had. And although I saw them come in here—and rare, that—they turned it to something 'cause they was something. Now, you cogitate that, my friend."

Art had a dozen invectives swirling and percolating in his mind, but they stuck in his throat as Mr. Stone fixed him for the longest minute Art had felt since—well, since now.

Plunk.

"Foregrip."

Plunk.

"Receiver and buttstock."

Mr. Stone put both hands on the gun parts and slid them forward. He then re-lit the old cigar with the most banged-up Zippo ever and drew deeply as Art said, "Thank you" in no more a whisper from a contrite boy.

A cloud of smoke enveloped them with Stone's exhale. "Come here."

"Sir?"

Another cloud of smoke.

"Closer."

The pawn broker seemed fifty feet away. Then came the sound in Art's ear: "Go home. You've been waiting long enough."

And...

[SHIFT]

Art put the two pieces of gun in the truck on the seat, cranked the truck, put it in gear, pulled out of the parking lot, and caught Mr. Stone's waving as he locked up the pawn shop, then...

[SHIFT]

proceeded to turn off the store's lights.

Back in the inventory room, Stone stopped and stared at the man slumped in the corner. A half-smoked yet snuffed cigar lay on his chest. He dozed with something of a smile on his face as he dreamed of himself standing there.

Then the person standing shivered — watery illusion evaporating to nothing as the slender form of Eva the witch materialized via her whispered sortilege.

"Thanks." The witch leaned close to whisper in his ear. "And no hard feelings."

She straightened, turned, and stepped through a misty portal in the wall and into the growing dusk over Fogle County. She sent herself into a passing raven and made straight for home.

EPILOGUE
INDEED, THEY ARE ONE

SATURDAY MORNING HAD COME AS THOUGH FRIDAY EVENING had passed in some slippery mystery. Art hadn't thought he'd been so tired yesterday after getting back from his dealings in town. He couldn't say he even recalled coming home—and him sober on top of it all. After a quick breakfast and a half-pot of coffee in his mug, he went outside and fiddled and fought with the tractor and getting the augur bit hooked up to the tractor. He saw at the shed where James had dropped off all those pecan saplings, and there were a helluva lot of them needing plenty of holes put in the dirt. Not a bad Saturday project and small way to celebrate the place actually being his. It would be good work, if a bit tedious, and that would help him think and compose in his head. He could even work on writing tonight. Maybe call Vera. He climbed on the tractor, fired it up, and pulled out onto the back field.

At the edge of the road, he saw somebody walking along the shoulder and turn onto his property and wave at him. He waved back to C.V. and thought, *Well, he doesn't have my tools, but at least he showed.*

As Art heaved a sigh, the land sighed with him and seemed, for a moment, satisfied as he returned to auguring the field in preparation of planting the pecan tree saplings. Wind gusted against the field and the broomsage, nodding like a congregation of wizened

Pentecostals, and he thought he heard Eva at the treeline singing:

> *Bot, of alle that here bult, of Bretagyne kynges*
> *Ay was Arthur the hendest, as I haf herde telle.*

(Sir Gawain and the Green Knight, l. 25-26)

AFTERWORD

THE KERNEL THAT BEGAN AS "A MATTER OF ANACHRONISMS, Archetypal yet Curious in Their Implications" grew out of my wanting to, for the past several years, write some retelling of the Arthurian legend. With an invitation to submit a story for an issue of *Behind the Wainscot*, I soon found the impetus to begin writing. I thought writing a Southern magical realism story would be just about right; however, I fast realized the only way that would suit my tastes and do the story justice was to take a deconstructionist approach.

It just clicked, as the ambiguous "they" say.

The images and scenes and bits of dialogue came, and I allowed myself the latitude of an intuitive approach to writing the rough draft. Then I filled in the gaps during revision, etc., etc. The challenge for me was to write what I hoped was an accessible story first with a simple premise: A man has pawned a family heirloom and wants to get it back. Add complications with some family and friends and a dose of magical realism, and away we go...

So, I had to construct the story in such a way that someone could read it, totally unaware of anything Arthurian, and come away feeling satisfied. Then I had to layer the references and situations enough that it would still be apparent that, hey-ho, here's a bit of Arthuriana that comes all shaken up (not stirred, thank you kindly).

The images came first. Excalibur became a double-barreled shotgun with engraving on its barrels and passed down through a couple three generations in the Penderton family. The Holy Grail transformed into one of those handy truck stop super-massive coffee mugs that, once purchased, you usually get to refill for free—a sure 'nough big mug, as we say down here. The Table Round morphed into one of those large utility line spools which folks sometimes use as tables on the cheap and make for some great lawn furniture of the rural variety in the South. And let us not forget Camelot as a single-wide trailer at the tail-end of some farm property and, yes, near a very nice five-acre pond.

The Pendragons chose to reveal themselves as Luther and Art Penderton, respectively. I don't give Gawain or Lancelot much page time, but they do show up as Wayne and Lance. Guinevere became Vera while Nyneve exposed herself as the neighborly witch across the pond from Art's property. No Merlin, I'm afraid. However, anyone fond of Perceval should be relieved to learn that dear ol' C.V. Deal is none other than Perceval himself. Since there's enough Arthuriana out there regarding his relationship to the Fisher King/Wounded King, I had to give a tip of the hat to said crippled ruler as Old Man Fisher, who instead of being wounded by a spear was wounded more innocently and accidentally with a frog gig. The brief digression in which Art and C.V. visit a certain Morgan [le Fay], there must needs be a fabulous creature, so the Questing Beast became that gigantic albino rattlesnake.

With the family heirloom, and Art's determination to retrieve it, I had latitude to play off the sword in the stone—Stone's pawn shop with Excalibur stuck, as it were, in the inventory. Once all the situations gelled, the simplest and most satisfying resolution I allowed myself (and the story and Art) was the planting of the pecan saplings to recognize that Art had gotten his act together and to highlight the old idea of Arthur's connection to the land and vice versa.

And here I'll close this perhaps not so brief afterword and take a moment to say thank you for your trip through some Southern magical realism and bumping into an old familiar friend in good ol' Art Penderton and walking with me through the two-path roads and along the fence lines and near the old oak hollow of the poem "Old Language."

—Berrien C. Henderson

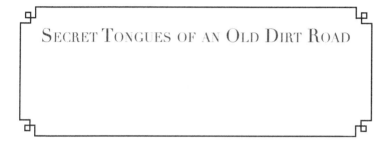

Secret Tongues of an Old Dirt Road

1

The dirt road unspooled
With our thoughts as we rode
Back to distant haunts:
Childhood at the old farm.

Now time—how time—had claimed
The yard and encroached, covetously,
The lime-tinged siding of the house.
Cedar trees crowded perspective;
Moss clung to old paths.

Even the dirt road had cut closer
To the front yard—

How memory, too, skews geography,
Abuts cobblestones once so familiar
To our shuffling feet.

2

We were certain, despite the planted pines
Stolid in the backyard,
Certain of the pear and fig trees.

"Just 'bout imagine they're there."

They are there.

Still.

At least the magnolia stood sentinel--
My watchtower from monkey-days,
The childhood days before uplifting.

3

You conjured recollection:
The rosebush,
Encircled by meteorites,
Claimed from new-harrowed earth.

     They had traveled the dark spaces,
     Roamed and burnt, their skins melted,
     Cosmological secrets fused by friction,
     Sealed in the ferrous esoterica.

     They, tumbling and slamming and forgotten
     For a time and times
     In the dark places of the earth.

Dredged up and placed amid drifting mists
Parting yet briefly as we dug
Fingers into the alluvia of reminiscence.

4

There are songs in the coverts
Of that rotting farmhouse,
Secrets just at the porch's edge,
Something cut off, whispered,
At the tongue of a cobbled walkway,
Its tip avulsed, gouged by the ditch
And numbed by the dribblings
Of anonymous beer cans.

Though never truly stopping,
We rode on—

"Yes, yes, this is the same road."

"Look, there are still goats at our
Eldest cousin's place."

Going forward we have returned,
Smiling in quiet.
The mist came back.

We rode—

"Let me take it in," you said.
"To remember."

5

I will show you the land,
And you will drive, pulling me along,
Urging and coaxing me forward, too,
Just as you had when pulling
The toy farmhouse and toy cow
While I crawled after it, and you.

So, I followed. And wondered.

And in my wondering asked the old man:

"What about those meteorites?"

"Just sandstone. Only sandstone."

Yes, but pushed up from the dark places
Of the earth—pinched and crushed and tumbled,
Extruded by the crust's slow-shifting
And the callused hands of men
We only know by their long stares
From out of black and white photographs,
From out of the oral traditions
That swap meteorite for sandstone
As they swapped generations' of dirt under fingernails,
Or drank and gambled their way out,
Or walked to the treeline "for a while"
To return home under a sheet—
One less bullet in the gun.

For the railroad and the military,
College and steelworkers and babies

Until the fields that made them,
Sustained them,

Extrude only wildflowers and weeds and memories
That nudge the ditch of a tongue of dirt road,
Speaking its glossolalia
Of mist, grayscale reminiscence:

You had said to help you find the road...

"Let me take it in...
"To remember."

FOLK UNSTUCK AND HAUNTED
BY CREATURES PARLOUS STRANGE

1
No Charms from across the Ocean

Before Old Man Fisher saw the black dogs, he heard their yowls, plaintive moans offered up to forgotten ur-gods. He braced in the door jamb of his back porch as the security light in the corner of the yard flickered off and was at best unreliable, and this evening he wished it would come back on. His left leg—what remained—ached against the prosthetic's plastic-and-leather cup. The leg itself was wooden and had taken him the better part of a year to carve and brace and bracket and hinge. Sometimes he still felt the persistent, dense phantom of his old leg through the wood. Ever since he'd lost the limb and nursed the purple-pink stump toward some tolerable level of ache instead of shrieking sensitivity, ever since then. From before then.

Not again.

He could've gone all day and night not seeing the black dogs.

Under the blue-sown specter of gibbous moonlight, three fluid patches of shadow weaved amongst themselves. They snuffled and yowled every now and then. Orange-red eyes like glowing embers shone in the night.

The *cusith* halted at the edge of the field where the two-path road bisected Old Man Fisher's property. They were velvet midnight come down from the dead space between stars.

He could not trust his dreams tonight, he knew. No amount of latches and locks on the trailer doors (or charms his grandmother had brought from across the ocean) would stay their influence — ghosts and whispers and shadow-things from of old, from land to land.

Their yipping struck out like laughter — taunts and ur-vulpine braggadocio to clabber a seventy-three-year-old man's marrow and make that phantom leg eager to move.

The wooden leg's brace creaked. The black dogs looked up and bayed an old song at the firmament's gulf so wide between Abraham and Lazarus.

Just like that, they vanished into a yawning wall of treeline shadow.

Fisher did an awkward hitch-turn, the dead *tok-tok-tokking* of the prosthetic leg accompanying him across the wood-slatted porch.

Inside he opened a cabinet door, and three old friends waited: Jack Daniels, Johnny Walker, and Southern Comfort. He grabbed the half-empty pint of Jack, then sat in his recliner and took off his wooden leg. It *klonked* over and hit his crutches — a clatter of metal and wood. No matter. He wasn't going anywhere but to the hot-smooth spirits-land of blurred and blunted and drift-away places. Places where they wouldn't be nipping the fringes of his psyche, just snuffling 'round the gulfs of his amber solace through the lonely hours that night.

2
NOT QUITE *IN MEDIA RES*, BUT CLOSE

LATER THAT NIGHT DREAMS CAME, AND HE WAS YOUNG AGAIN. He found himself in a stand of planted pines bordered and girded by firebreaks amid the hectares of longleaf pines. The .30-30 he'd bought at fourteen was there. He'd posted miles of property, even done some trapping here and there, to scrimp and save for that gun.

"You work. You earn. You save," his daddy had said.

"Yes, sir," he had said.

The gun flickered from color to monochrome to sepia until Fisher picked it up. He set it back down and looked at the ladder stand, all old and rusty, leaning on the pine tree. It should not have been there, like the gun. Yet.

"Jarvis."

The woman with a mane of raven tresses came around a corner in the firebreak. She, too, flickered, but more like a television screen with faulty analog reception.

"I know you," he said. He felt so young again and reached a hand out to her. His hand was no longer leathery and liver-spotted and confirmed his youth-in-dream. "You live —"

She slid in behind him and clutched him back-to-chest. Her breath came warm on the nape of his neck. "I need you to see something," she said, her mouth at his ear. He thought for a moment her hair would reach out and suffocate him.

A ghost amid the splayed palmetto fronds and bunched-up, huddling wax myrtles, flashes of white eased across the pine rows. Where another firebreak intersected this one and—

"Didn't I tell you once before you weren't invited here?" said Fisher.

"We aren't quite where you think," she said.

"You're a witch."

"I am many things, that among them."

The white deer stepped onto the break. Only a hand-sized black patch stood out on its shoulder. Fisher counted thirteen tines on the rack, the antlers furry with summer velvet, blood-engorged and feeding the growth of those magnificent tines each to each.

He turned to the woman who was not his wife or anyone else to him. "Why are you here?" He toed the ground with a boot tip and cut a curving furrow.

"Now, why would you do that?" said the witch.

"Read once that circumscription helps in such situations," he said.

"As impressed as I am at your seeming reading habits, I'm already here," she said. "Already in."

"This is a dream."

"No, you haven't woken from the Other yet, Jarvis," she said.

The deer snorted at them and ghosted away.

She let go of Fisher and had the gun in her hands and blurred the intervening feet to the tree and gun. Fisher felt a sudden absence of density as she did so. From barrel to receiver, she smoothed a hand over the metal; Fisher couldn't make out what she whispered, but everywhere her skin touched metal, etchings appeared—vine motifs interwoven amid leaf patterns. She sang, too, and Fisher's heart cried for her to stop because the song was the most exquisite he'd ever heard, and he knew it would end, would be the coda for this Other place that she claimed was no dreamscape.

"You might need this—the glamour of it," she said.

"Just what the hell'd you do to my gun?" he said.

"Remember when, even with this, your own gun, your daddy only gave you one bullet to take hunting?" Her voice wavered, and out of her plum-lipped mouth came a ghost's voice: "'One bullet. Sometimes you can't afford to miss.'"

"You need to leave," he said, flat-voiced.

"When you get your gun, come tell me it was a dream, Jarvis Pelham Fisher," she said.

She pointed.

He looked down.

His left leg was gone below the knee though he himself was fourteen again. The physics of this place afforded him the luxury of balance and painlessness.

As she walked into the shadows of the planted pines, Fisher tried to get to his gun, but he found himself as rooted to the ground as the surrounding trees. The earth buckled beneath the gun and tipped it from where it leaned against the tree. Roots burst from the loam and wrapped and encased the carbine and subsumed it in some arboreal cocoon, then thrashed along the ground, making straightway for the stump of Fisher's leg.

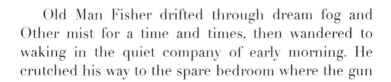

Old Man Fisher drifted through dream fog and Other mist for a time and times, then wandered to waking in the quiet company of early morning. He crutched his way to the spare bedroom where the gun

was and ran his hand over the vine-and-leaf etchings;
the metal felt warm. No, he thought. Not warm but
imbued with Eva's glamour—witching unction from
an eld sister to matrons of earth and water and fire and
wind, inheritor of such dominion as sun and moon and
stars allow their children who hear best and learn their
songs.

Fisher worked the lever and checked the chamber:
one round.

What the hell did you do to my gun?

Soft, the whining outside the trailer. A gentle pad-
pad-padding even on the roof, and he followed the
sounds, tracked them with the gun's muzzle.

Mischievous yip-yipping.

Red eyes floated at the forefront of the living shadow
coming down the hallway.

Old Man Fisher put buttstock to shoulder and
chambered the round. The black dog lowered its head
and curled its lips in a mute snarl, then walked through
the walls to join its brethren.

Only Fisher, old one-legged man that he was, and
a gun.

Then the quiet and no sleep.

At least predawn had begun lighting the east.

3
LIKE THE SEASONS, THE RECURSION OF MEMORY COMES 'ROUND

FISHER HADN'T ALWAYS LIVED THERE ON THE OLD WASDIN property. For nearly forty years he'd lived only a few miles away on down the long tongue of clay road and past a couple of oak hills on a nice two-acre plot with rose bush frontage because she'd liked that along with the grapevine trellises in the side yard. There was a tiny yet serviceable creek not a quarter mile distant.

Children came and grew, and the seasons and years carved their tributaries upon the Fishers, and something more upon her, and he lost her except the pangs at spring when the roses came back, and later in the summer he would make some homemade wine from the grapes out of his own yard and bury the bottles in the backyard, in the cool loam back near the corner.

The house had burned.

He'd just finished dropping off other people's children and made the long swing 'round back to his property. The volunteer fire department was there just to keep it from spreading through the yard.

That night he dug up a bottle of wine and drank and slept in his truck. It was the first night, too, the *cusith* had come rippling down the road, baying softly the closer they came to the edge of his ruined property.

Over that long weekend, he picked through the ashes and washed up with the hand pump at the shed.

He was glad he'd kept that shallow well. Family and friends offered shelter, clothes. No, he'd said. They deferred and let him grieve for the second time in his adult life. There was a pile of barrels in the grass from his burned-up guns; only his childhood rifle, having been in the truck, survived. One picture of his wife. Pregnant with their first child.

He used the insurance money to buy and convert an old one-room schoolhouse down the road. He kept a wood-burning stove for the winter and a window unit in the summer and parked the school bus at the old place, only a quarter-mile down the road.

For the next several years, he might see the black dogs in the early morning and racing alongside the bus until his first pick-up. One time, he had seen a solitary *cusith* coming to the water's edge at a creek; the black dog bayed once, pawing the smooth-running, tea-dark tannin water, then vanished back into the dappling shadows of the hollow. He feared them the way a man fears weapons or fire—respect, caution, enough mistrust to account for those wild moments none may anticipate.

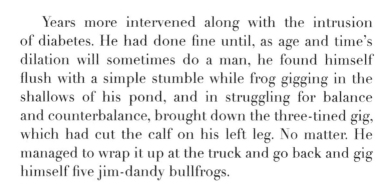

Years more intervened along with the intrusion of diabetes. He had done fine until, as age and time's dilation will sometimes do a man, he found himself flush with a simple stumble while frog gigging in the shallows of his pond, and in struggling for balance and counterbalance, brought down the three-tined gig, which had cut the calf on his left leg. No matter. He managed to wrap it up at the truck and go back and gig himself five jim-dandy bullfrogs.

But cleaning up at home just wasn't the same as it should've been, and the modals of accidents spin out unintended consequences, especially to drunk old diabetics with an inches-long gash on a calf.

From out of the fog of trauma and opiate haze and the lingering tendrils of anesthesia, he had seen them at the door of his hospital room all the way in Savannah at Memorial Medical. The black dogs only wavered, even as nurses walked through the *cusith*'s shadow-forms (perhaps pausing at a slight shiver).

They'd only left when C.V. Deal and C.V.'s Papa Eustace had come to visit. Not long after that, Eustace Deal had passed.

Five years gone, both old man and black dogs.

Old Man Fisher would've much rather seen the former.

4
The Heat That Billows off Everything

He'd been down about C.V.'s absence—the young man not having visited in some weeks now--but didn't begrudge him a young man's time and latitude and mobility. Plus, it was 'bout too hot to be gallivanting as mid-August asserted itself along the verdant, claustrophobic backroads of Fogle County. Fisher loathed the next electric bill, what with the AC's never cutting off. Even too hot to hit the sauce, and that made it all so wrong, nearly blasphemous.

Fisher hobbled out to his backyard. A respite had come; yesterday had brought a mad-dog line of thunderstorms. Where the low nineties had dominated by seven or eight o'clock, the eighties prevailed, praise God and baby Jesus. Nothing like that lasted this time of year, so it was best to enjoy. Evening's deep magenta dome buttressed a host of scattered mare's tails. After a while the Perseids began cutting icy furrows in the infant night.

He heard the throaty, phlegmatic rumblings of the old pickup truck before he saw it turning down his drive, and he recognized both driver and vehicle and got up to limp to the back porch. A wave of gassy and oily smells buffeted him as the driver shut off the truck, which shimmied with a kind of death-rattle even as C.V. Deal poured himself out of the driver's side. He pulled a small cooler out of the bed and held it up.

"Hey, Old Man," he said.

"C.V., good to see you," said Fisher.

"Good to be seen. You had supper yet?"

"No, not yet. Was on the verge of skipping it."

"You got any grits?"

"Am I breathing?"

"Fixings for hush puppies?"

"By God."

"Well, I guess it's a party," said C.V. He came and clapped Fisher on the shoulder and quickly opened the cooler. "Lookee. Three catfish I just caught down to the Pendertons' pond."

"Well, C.V., I reckon that will be a better supper than Southern Comfort," said Fisher.

"You ought to hold off that," said C.V.

"How I made it this far in life without a minder is beyond me," said Fisher.

"I was wondering the same thing," said C.V.

"You coming?"

"Sure."

As they went inside, a handful of meteors scraped the night sky while at the treeline the black dogs bayed, but Fisher ignored them.

It was good to have some company.

"Why do you keep coming 'round, C.V.?" said Old Man Fisher. He checked the grits.

"You keep feeding me. I'm like a stray," said C.V. "Besides, I'm supposed to."

"Figure it's your Christian duty?"

"That's a helluva thing, saying it like that," said C.V. "Gave Papa my word. I ain't got much, Old Man, but I got *that* much."

Fisher stirred the grits, then sat down. "I miss your Papa Eustace."

"Me, too."

"Done took my insulin this morning, by the by. Knew you'd hector me about it."

"Yes, sir. You all right?"

"Just thinking. Ready for cooler weather. Fall and such."

"That's a tall order and a long wait," said C.V.

"Squirrels and rice would be nice," said Fisher.

"Well, go and get you some. Plink 'em out the pecan orchard."

"Be ate up with parasites 'til first frost. Like I said — long way off."

"Deer'll be moving by then, too," said C.V. "I ain't been hunting in a while."

"Been a long time for me."

"You know, I bet you could lay up in those old faring pens and benchrest shoot off a rail," said C.V.

"You're hell on a good idea every now and then," said Fisher.

"It's a gift."

Fisher checked the hush puppies and set them on a plate layered with paper towels, which absorbed the grease in strange trans fat Rorschach patterns. He turned off the Fry Daddy while C.V. worked the delicate dance of frying the catfish in a skillet in the constrained kitchen space. Still, it was worth sweating over food, and fresh food at that. An oscillating fan nearby consistently proved its impotence.

"I could whip up some French fries, you want," said C.V.

"Ain't got no taters. You've been kindly enough, Son," said Fisher. "Where you been lately?"

"Helped dry in some duplexes down to Brunswick for a few weeks. Good work while it lasted. They needed a few extra hands, so I went. At least I got low overhead like you."

"You ought to be off doing something more," said Old Man Fisher.

"I know."

They fixed their plates and sat at a little card table with mismatched chairs.

"You batter fish like your Papa used to."

"Yes, sir."

Silence for a time.

"Thanks for coming." Fisher picked at some bones on his plate and finished off his third hush puppy.

"Yes, sir."

"Sure you don't want a drink?" said Fisher.

"No disrespect, but you sure you should be doing that, what with your diabetes?"

"It's my liver's more in danger."

"Well, you know what I mean."

"Yeah, I do. 'preciate the thought."

"Yes, sir."

Old Man Fisher got up and gripped C.V.'s shoulder for some additional support, then went to his recliner and plopped down. He pulled out a pint of Jack Daniels from a warped magazine rack as C.V. began cleaning up.

"You good?" said Fisher.

"I got the kitchen."

"You'll make somebody a good wife one day."

"Ha ha ha."

"Thanks, C.V."

"Anytime, Old Man."

Yep, thought Fisher as he pulled on the pint of ol' No. 7. Sure was good to have human company.

5
THE VAST GULFS OF OLD TIME

OLD MAN FISHER FLUSHED WITH THE ANTICIPATION OF getting out to the old faring pens with C.V. after their talk, especially now that September had encroached its autumnal way upon the end of a long summer. He surveyed his property with the long acres of pasture stretching down to the corner of live oaks where the land dipped into a full-blown hollow, just a strip of planted pines for wind breaks at the field's edge. He believed C.V. had called it rightly. Those faring pens part way down the pasture would be the best place to lay up, where they could set their rifles while sitting in fold-out camping chairs. The long-since-whitened tines of years' and years' worth of bucks' antlers all tacked beneath the eaves mocked the time and years he hadn't hunted.

Off the back porch was just a bit much no matter how good Fisher's eyesight was. Plus, the ballistics of the .30-30 wouldn't allow it, and damned if he knew what Eva had done to the gun. No matter. Or less matter. He drank.

Late evening fire painted the tail-end of the property. The small pond in the far corner had an overflow ditch instead of a spillway and worked its way to the creek beyond. The creek ran deep into the oaks with plenty of deer runs and miscellaneous game trails.

Fisher had put meat on the table many a time, keeping the chest freezer full sometimes, but it had been too long since he'd hunted. He had never really needed much meat—just an old widower with an occasional hankering for marinated backstraps or a Dutch oven of chili. Fishing took up most of his time, and he had the trimmed-down milk jugs frozen and full of panfish to prove it—good to trade for fresh fruits and vegetables or swap for some peach wine from time to time. Fisher had a sudden craving for grilled deer sausage and made his decision.

Then the albino buck came out of the treeline at the gnarled live oak. Head down, then up. Looking. Back down. Tail a-flicker. The white hide shone in the sun and stood in sharp contrast to the browns of the buck's tentative companions, some does and spike bucks— all flickering tails themselves and eager to forage. They worked their way toward the field adjacent his property—a sprawling five-hundred acres flush now with peanuts ready for early October harvest. The deer disappeared for a time behind the low rise in the field, then back in view on their way to the back rows.

The shadow of the trailer and outbuildings spilled far into the backyard, then merged with the pregnant twilight, rendering the deer to their Platonic forms along with the rest of the land, and first magnitude stars revealed their witness from the vast gulfs of old time and the outer dark.

The deer froze at once, then sprint-bounded to the treeline and were followed by the baying of hounds, but no one Fisher knew had hounds or Walker dogs that'd just run free; no one was so careless as that. No. He knew. Denial was a stupid commodity for an old man to think he could afford.

Midnight patches loped in the dusk. They veered from the treeline, and their baying and barking grew softer the closer they came to Old Man Fisher's place until there was only their silence, their obsidian presence, the conviction of their lambent red eyes upon him.

"Don't come no closer."

They did, though, paws hovering just above the grasses. Occasionally came the wafting of burnt-grass odors where their paws had touched down. They wavered like oil-slick reflections of ur-dogs from out of earliest nightmares. The *cusith* snuffled the back steps, then spun and raced into the infant night.

After a while, Old Man Fisher worked himself with great effort back inside. Sleep came hard and deep on the heels of spirited comfort and into glammed-over dream kingdoms, Other kingdoms, memories from what seemed another life.

6
Other-Talk

When C.V. Deal had dropped by again, Old Man Fisher had hollered for him to come on in and found the man just staring at the antique gun.

"Them's mighty fancy engravings," said C.V. "What'd you do to it?"

"I didn't. She did."

"She who?"

"Nina Faye Evangeline."

"Hmmmmm."

"Yep. We need to take her some fish," said Old Man Fisher. He let C.V. inspect the .30-30.

"Want me to get some out the chest freezer on the back porch?" said C.V.

"I was thinking maybe fresher than that," said Fisher.

"Offering?"

"No, C.V. Just reciprocating."

"With fish."

"With fish."

"Here I thought you done that with fractions and such," said C.V.

Old Man Fisher chuckled. "Sometimes in relationships."

"With witches."

"With witches."

C.V. proffered the gun to Fisher and said, "I'll go get the rods and reels."

"Good idea."

The battered F-150 jounced and creaked down the
path from the far edge of the Penderton place. Ripples
from breams and other such panfishess' popping had
scribed and ciphered sine waves across the delicate
membrane of the five-acre pond. The old man saw a
kingfisher plunge, then zip away.

Eva's small house with its wide front porch
beckoned, and she sat reading in the porch swing.
Old Man Fisher parked the truck, got his cane and the
frozen jug of fish. After a bit of wriggling and not a
little cussing, he was out of the truck. The hinge of the
wooden leg creaked. Morning held shadows close in
this nook of property overlooking its Piscean demesne.
The playing breeze kept bugs at bay.

Eva closed the book but kept swinging. "Good
morning, Jarvis."

"Eva. Mind I come on the porch?"

She indicated a wicker chair. "Please do. Wouldn't
want to bar a guest, now, would we?"

"Thanks." He set down the jug of fish.

"It's been a while since you've wandered down this
way," said Eva.

"I could say the same of you," he said.

As she grinned, her pupils shuddered, tilted to
vertical, then back to normal. "Just a bit of a visit."

"Beg to differ, Eva. A visitation. Didn't really
appreciate it, nor your messing with my property."

"You mean your gun."

"Well, that and the getting to it."

"There are... ways around getting around," said
the witch. The book faded, its color bleeding until it
vanished. It was where the jug had been, the jug now
nearer the swing. "See?"

"You can have them."

"Implicit in your bringing them."

"The same."

A red-tailed hawk called from its winging progress over the treetops. It gyred in the nearby field, then with backswept wings plunged amid the hay. Mouse in talons, the hawk returned to the treeline and fed.

"So, what else is it, Jarvis?" said Eva.

"Figured you could tell me," he said.

"How so?"

"You went through an awful lot of trouble to bring strange ministrations to my gun and dreams, woman. To an old man with one good leg nearly as busted as the gun itself."

"Hardly busted," she said.

"Well?"

"You'll have the one shot to get your answer," she said. "Or maybe not."

"I've always appreciated your knack for getting to the point, Eva."

Her laughter glittered in the morning air. She stood, and with each step blurred, paused, turned back age and time until she conjured herself into the woman in Old Man Fisher's dreams. She touched the wooden leg. "I could have healed you." The wood vibrated. "Had you come."

"You keep on, and I might just."

"You are a dirty old man."

"To such as know me, or think they do," said Fisher. "Well, I best get going."

"You just got here," said Eva. She picked up the book and handed it to him. "Here, an even trade. Thank you for the fish, Jarvis."

He turned the book over in his liver-spotted hands, then flipped through it. "I read some Chretien de Troyes before," he said.

"When?"

His eyes looked past her for a thousand yards—a thousand years. "Well, I heard it somewhere, I reckon."

"You want it?"

"Maybe something more recent," he said.

The book warmed in his palms and flickered through sepia and monochrome then back to colors rich and dense.

Old Man Fisher said, "Been a while since I read any Hemingway."

"Maybe it will keep your mind off other things," said Eva.

"What other things?"

"Things that slip in during the night. Lurking padfoots and the like."

"Like witches?" said Fisher.

Her eyes turned from flint to iceberg-blue. "I think you know exactly what I mean. Your old friends."

"Ain't my friends."

"But they are old and persistent, are they not, on their wild hunts?"

"Yes."

"Good day, Mr. Fisher."

"Good-bye, Eva."

As he hobbled back down to his truck, he couldn't help thinking how talking to that woman during waking time wasn't too far removed from dream-talk. Or Other-talk. Or whatever it was.

Her singing followed him and distracted his frustrated thoughts with syrup and sunshine and talk of green things—electuaries laced with glamour.

For a while, he thought maybe he'd accomplished something.

Just what, he wasn't sure.

7
TAUNTS

A FEW DAYS OF C.V.'S BEING GONE TO PARTS UNKNOWN, AND Fisher could've used him. At least it seemed only to take a stray thought for the young man to show.

"Where'd you get the book?" said C.V.

"Had it these days to pass the time," said Fisher.

"It was more a location question than a time one."

"A bit of a swap, you might say."

"Ain't too keen on trading with witches, even it if is Hemingway."

"What of his have your read?"

"Just about all of them Nick Adams stories."

"Name some, then," said Fisher.

"What? Are you suddenly quizzing me?" said C.V.

"Appears so. Quit dissembling, Son."

"'Big-Two Hearted River' and 'Indian Camp.'"

"That's two."

"That's right, Old Man. You said 'some,' and that's got to be plural, and, by God, two's plural enough, way I see it," said C.V.

"A self-styled scholar, and sure 'nough master of the King's English, and I never knew it," said Fisher.

"Well, I wouldn't go so far as that."He indicated Fisher's book. "You read the one about the hyenas yet?"

"Yep."

"I'd like to read it again," said C.V. "Almost done with two Louis L'Amour books I could swap you for."

"Which ones?" said Fisher.

"*Yondering*. And that poetry collection."

"He ain't wrote no poetry."

"Like hell he ain't," said C.V. "Just like Hemingway wrote some."

"C.V. Deal, you can say too much sometimes."

"I got some learning to show for my education," he said. "How 'bout yourself?"

Old Man Fisher flashed up three fingers. "Then I suppose you can read between the lines."

"Just tell me what you want from Duke's short order grill since I'm buying."

They both froze at a *ta-tump-tumping* on the back porch, then a *whomp-clatter* outside, and C.V. checked it quick and stared a moment.

"What is it?" said Fisher.

"Who you know 'round here with a bunch of dogs running loose?" said C.V.

"Nobody."

"Well, they're sure as hell chasing that coon that was just outside your porch. Anyhow, what'd you say you wanted from the short order grill?"

Fisher got a faraway look in his eyes. "No, C.V. I'm good."

"What about eating?"

"Ain't hungry no more."

"All right. Your stomach, not mine," said C.V.

"You going to be gone long?" said Fisher.

"Don't suspect so."

"Coming back here?"

"I reckon."

Fisher offered a noncommittal *hmmmmm* as C.V. left. He waited for C.V. to get to his truck before he eased to the window and watched him pull off. Away in the field across the highway, half a dozen *cusith* raced across the furrows, and Old Man Fisher thought he heard their taunting yips in his head.

8
WITH FROST COME FIENDISH SPIRITS

OFTEN ENOUGH FISHER KEPT ODD HOURS. IT STRUCK HIM TO clonk and hobble into the kitchen to check the drugstore calendar on the corkboard near the refrigerator when he could see the phases of the moon for himself and trust his old bones, and sometimes he himself wondered what good it did him. Hell, he thought, old age was keeping up with him more than he it, and what good, really, were some more X's on a grid?

Fisher had always waited 'til the first frost to do his hunting. Even when squirrel season came in August, it was best to wait for the first frost to kill the parasites. Where deer were concerned, it was a matter of migratory eating patterns—a dance of storm and moon and season and beast. Now that late October asserted itself with a hard frost two days gone he'd make sure to call C.V.

Fall had always invigorated him, and he thought maybe it was coming off the nigh-tropical summer and the land reclaiming itself from the verdant, self-imposed claustrophobia. He most enjoyed the crisp, clear nights, and his eyes were still sharp enough he could let his mind and sight wander while the constellations toiled through the night and with scant regard for Fisher and the rest of humanity.

On the back porch he checked some clothes on the short clothesline, and the nippiness had dried them

off just fine, thank you, as the cool breeze tousled
the chambray work shirt and dungarees, and Fisher
considered them husks of himself swaying on the line
as he hobbled to the backyard and had a drink from a
banged-to-hell flask.

Tonight frost would return. Fisher felt it in his
bones and the stump of his left leg. Settling in an old
camping chair, he sipped some Southern Comfort
and cocked his head at the thick toenail clipping of a
crescent moon, which by his mark would have the deer
moving out in the shadow of the treeline before long.

"You'll catch your death of cold out here." Eva's
voice sidled up to him from across the yard. The
security lamp flickered.

Fisher held up his flask. "Already self-medicating
against it."

"Can I come over?"

"You may."

"Ah, been studying grammar."

"Hadn't thought of her in years." He smiled at Eva's
pealing laughter. "At least you asked this time instead
of waiting 'til I feel asleep."

"We've been over this before."

"You brought them black dogs."

Eva said, "*Those* black dogs. And you're wrong. I got
little truck with or sway over such as the *cusith*, who
keep their own counsel as they travel the secret paths,
and they come for whomever they want."

Fisher pulled from the flask. "See, that's the problem.
They been sniffing around me a long, long time."

Eva perked up. "Perhaps they found something
they like."

"If they like jerky, I suppose."

"You're getting tight," said Eva.

"My flask's broken and must needs repairing," said Fisher, turning it upside down. "Besides, the night is young."

"Cold, too."

Fisher got up and breathed heavily enough to watch a plume drift between him and Eva.

"Not so far into my drink this evening that I don't know when somebody's fishing for an invitation."

"You're a hard old man," she said.

"Flattery'll get you nowhere," he said. "Besides, if you wanted it bad enough, you'd just as soon enter through the Other, right, Eva? More your style."

She cast invectives in strange tongues as his back.

"Eva, you can say all you want in Latin and French," said Old Man Fisher. "Answer's still the same."

"Bastard."

"Most times I'd agree. Tonight, especially."

He felt the gust of wind from her flight and swirl as she spirited herself away.

Tonight was lonelier than he'd have wished, even in his dreams.

9
SALLY FORTH THE TWAIN

C.V. HAD BROUGHT AN OLD SAVAGE .243 WITH A STOCK 3x9 Bushnell scope. No telling when or for what he'd traded it.

"Mighty fine gun you got there," Fisher had said when C.V.'d shown up.

"Had it a while," said C.V.

"Talking 'bout that Peacemaker with which you're about to clean up the town."

"Papa's. Remember how he'd carry it with him sometimes?" said C.V.

"I do." How time had abandoned portions of memory already!

"You should've let me put out bait corn," said C.V.

"Deer've been feeding and don't—I'd hazard—need our help."

"Wouldn't have been much. Just put some about a hundred yards away from the faring pens."

"You can't shoot with that scope?"

"Says the man with iron sights."

"My eyes are old. And fine," said Fisher. "Besides, I've forgotten more about hunting than you know."

"You'll shit, too, you eat regular."

Fisher waved him hushed. "We best be quiet, now."

The breeze blew from out the oak hollow. In a few more hours it would be nice and crisp. From his porch the past few nights, Old Man Fisher had watched the deer move with the early moonrise each evening. Silence and discipline overtook the pair as they laid the barrels of their guns on an old rail after settling into their fold-out camping chairs. Their breath began fogging up as the shadows grew long against the earth, and the world seemed to forget itself in the slow movement of twilight on the land. From the crook in the land line where the giant live oak stood stolid at the one corner, movement caught their eyes. C.V. eased his rifle's buttstock to the hollow of his shoulder and peered through the scope. Fisher already knew it was the albino buck. C.V. waited until the deer moved farther out from the treeline and turned full-broadsided, and Fisher appreciated the youth's patience for a good shot.

He heard him stilling his breath as the buck dropped his head to begin foraging. That it was the albino and such a huge buck didn't seem to matter to C.V., but Fisher suspected as much.

C.V. cocked his head a moment, adjusting his eyesight against the scope's reticle. At least the wind still favored them, and C.V. slowed his breathing and eased the slack out of the trigger. In between a heartbeat and a breath, C.V. Deal squeezed the .243's trigger, and the rifle recoiled with smooth, controlled familiarity against his shoulder. He recovered muzzle control, racked the bolt, and sighted again down the fields even as Old Man Fisher saw the albino buck freeze, its legs buckling a bit, then digging in. It was never like the movies—a struck target being flung; in fact, the deer took a shaky bound and ran off.

"Let him run and bleed out some," said Fisher.

"Figured. I still got him," said C.V. "You wait, he'll hit the treeline and make a circle."

"Hope he don't try the hollow."

"He won't make it that far," said C.V. He knelt to recover and pocket the spent casing. "That's still a big bastard."

"Yep."

A minute or two later, and the buck came back out the treeline and stumbled.

"There he goes," said Fisher.

"Un-huh." C.V. sighted, then looked up and down the field, and re-sighted. "What the hell?"

Then Fisher heard what C.V. had seen.

The *cusith* swarmed out the shadows of the treeline. They had taken the buck to bay and came to the blood of his wounding. Their moans and baying reached Fisher and C.V.

"Oh, God, what is that?" said C.V. "They ain't coyotes."

"Black dogs."

"Whose?"

Fisher's mouth went dry. "We got to go."

"Get in the truck," said C.V. He hurried away and fired up the Ford and pulled around so that Old Man Fisher wouldn't have to walk so far.

They bumped and rattled to the far end of the field and piled out of the truck with their guns in hand. C.V. froze, though, at the front of the vehicle. Half a dozen pairs of red eyes stared up at the men as silver-fanged maws snapped the air, and just like that, gone. The albino buck bleated and shrieked and snorted only twenty yards away. C.V. shot again, and the animal slumped, then struggled again, fell quiet.

He and Fisher approached the deer.

"Hung up on that old barbed wire," said Fisher. The old broken fenceline had unspooled over the years, and the *cusith* had taken advantage of the deer's being trapped.

C.V. said, "Going to be an ironclad bitch to get ou—"

The buck came alive once more, blood all over its front shoulder and covering the black patch. Burnt marks from the touch of the black dogs marred its hide. The bit of fence constricting one hind leg uncoiled, and it fell to its fore-knees, then leaped forward, butting C.V. hard enough to send his rifle spinning and landing barrel-down in the soft field-dirt. C.V. pitched hard and brought up his arms as the fore-hooves came down; neither deer nor man made sound, and Old Man Fisher threw up his .30-30 but couldn't get a clear, safe shot for fear of hitting C.V.

No.

The deer butted again and partially lifted C.V., one bottom tine hanging in the youth's belt. The buck spun and pinned C.V. to an old tree stump, and that's when C.V. found his voice, crying out as tines punctured his belly. In only a few seconds the entire event unfolded, but to Fisher is seemed a repulsive lifetime.

The buck disengaged from C.V. and wheeled on the black dogs. As they swarmed once again, Old Man Fisher aimed and squeezed. Ethereal fire bloomed from the end of the barrel as the bullet sizzled through the air and slammed into the deer, buckling, and from the entry wound came a spray of gore and viscera out the exit wound—gouts of argent spider webbing from whatever glamour Eva had imbued the bullet. In its death throes, the deer bleated weakly, then uttered muffled, panicked sounds as the *cusith* overwhelmed the poor beast. Portions of its body melted away under the tear of their starlight fangs.

Old Man Fisher turned his attention to C.V. All he had to do was get the young man to the truck.

He underhooked one of C.V.'s arms and tried to haul him to his feet. Blood spilled and covered his shirtfront.

C.V. tried to stand, then crumpled under his own weight and nearly dragged Fisher down.

"Can't manage Old Ma—" And then C.V. passed slap out.

Fisher shouldn't have looked back, but the faraway growls and soft moans compelled him. But for the deer's dying, the *cusith* remained occupied, allowing Fisher time to haul poor, broken C.V.

The black dogs still crashed upon and swarmed the buck—obsidian waves with starlight-silver fangs and amber fire eyes. They offered no snapping of jaws or baying or growling now, just a mute feeding frenzy and spray of fluids and gobbets of viscera.

By the time Old Man Fisher was halfway to the truck, he thought of resting, yet the black dogs bayed softly, left off the deer's carcass, and began circling him and C.V.

Please wake up, C.V.

They came one at a time, nipping or with teeth bared in muffled growls, a sinister reticence spun out of shadowed origins. A pair of them barreled into Fisher and C.V., both pitching into the field grass. The old man cursed them and for his trouble met with the reward of having his prosthetic leg snatched off and dragged away. Now came the tiny, taunting yips and yowls. Fisher snatched the Peacemaker from C.V.'s belt and fired a blistering trifecta of .45's at the nearest *cusith*, which dissipated like oil drops on water, only to reform and hunch down for a lunge.

Eva's voice, some song from elsewhere (and here Fisher missed his grandmother as he heard it) insinuated itself over the field. Then came a litany of lilts and glottal stops and fricatives as the world and air warped around Old Man Fisher, and a murder of crows rippled from out the dark haunts of the treeline and swooped down, confusing the *cusith*.

He had never trusted dusk, the world with its bled-out colors, and either his old eyes turned astigmatic or the land had, and Eva's words returned to him.

"...haven't woken from the Other yet..."

Fisher didn't want to be caught in the dark, phantom leg returned or not. His mouth tasted awful, and he shoved down those thoughts as he pretended not to notice (but how wonderful to have back his leg! God, yes!) while he half-dragged, half-stumbled with C.V.'s unconscious body. The paltry momentum still carried them with a *fra-banging* into the front panel of the truck. Old Man Fisher wrenched open the passenger side door and after three attempts got the youth inside. C.V. moaned, and Old Man Fisher couldn't say as he blamed the young man, all things being equal. He bled from a hoof-strike gash on his head, tine puncture in his side just under the short ribs, more punctures in one of his forearms. Where one of the *cusith* had gotten to him, the exposed ankle flesh sported second degree burns.

Fisher tried not to think too hard about having carried the other man, especially since his leg was whole again—translucent and whole and damned-well not supposed to be there but he was damned-glad it was. The worst was the nipping of the *cusith* and thoughts of a renewed attack.

"Y'all may as well pack it up," said Old Man Fisher, firing up the decrepit Ford.

The black dogs pitched in and out of the headlights' beams like playful yet sinister puppies. Just a short

drive to the back porch. He could get to the phone; he
hoped so. The stump seared as it was wont to do when
the prosthetic's cup wasn't a good fit or like before
when the skin was so thin and tender.

Best have me a talk with that woman sometime 'bout this.
Amid the shock and pain, C.V. mumbled.

"Yeah, well, don't say I ain't never done you no
favors," said Fisher. God Almighty, but he could use a
drink—nothing stiff, just water, only a little something
to take the coppery taste from his mouth. He parked
the truck and poured himself out.

One of the black dogs had swung wide and stood
at the bottom of the back porch's steps and whispered
eldritch things in its *cusith* tongue.

"Maybe," said Old Man Fisher. "Maybe some other
time, ol' boy."

The black dog growled, its ears laying down.

"If you'd of wanted either of us, I figure you'd of
done more while you had a chance. Go find some other
food to play with."

He waved his arm and snapped his fingers.

"Get, I say!"

The black dog leaped forward and snapped at
Fisher's hand, then sniffed at C.V.'s blood dripping
from it. Old Man Fisher dropped his hand and on the
ground inscribed an arc in blood.

"Go on, now, you sumbitch."

The *cusith* whimpered, then made to lick the man's
hand, but Fisher drew back.

"No more."

The black dog spun and leaped away, tittering
almost hyena-like. As the *cusith* made another bound,
the security light came on, and the creature bled itself
away into a thin ribbon of midnight to pass through

the pool of illumination—this brother to darkness, sojourner of dusk, courser at twilight.

Fast in its wake came a bat, its flight a maddening gyre, uncertain orbital of moth-getting.

He thought he heard the bat's *ee-ree-eep-eep*, but it faded as it dodged unstuck spirits in the air. Eva detached herself from the night and called it forth, nuzzling this chiropteran familiar and clicking and *tsking* as she shimmered to mist, then back to her usual form. She hovered over C.V. in the cab of the truck and whispered.

"He can't speak for himself," said Fisher, collapsing just inside the porch. He forced himself up on an elbow and reached out for Eva, pointed at her—bloody hand of accusation in the autumn night, then upturned plea and waving. "Just go on in and call for help."

"Do you need your insulin?" said Eva.

"It'd help a good goddamned bit."

"I'll see what I can do," she said, "since you asked so nicely."

Maybe he'd kept his phone bill current, too, she thought, dragging C.V. out of the truck and inside the trailer.

EPILOGUE
THE CONVICTION OF THINGS DEAD AND GONE

FISHER TOOK HIS TIME HEADING ACROSS THE BACKYARD AND past the faring pens. The trek had seemed so much farther that night just getting to the truck. The brackets hardly squealed on the prosthetic leg, but the stump hurt. Fisher kept an eye on the sky as he trudged through the back pasture. Amid the hay grass nodded clumps of broom sage in the wind coming off the treeline. He sniffed the air.

The turkey buzzards hadn't circled even when a warm front had moved through, and Old Man Fisher wondered if the air and the sky above that corner of the field was now tainted. He had gone back down there only one other time in the intervening two weeks and seen the dead patches, the sere-ness from the *cusith*'s padding around. Only the buck's head and some ragged strips of carcass and the bones now existed; neither weather nor sun had touched that corpse. Maybe the cold. Only the cold, now it had returned. The empty eye sockets had convicted him with their hollow, Other staring and reminded him of the wild shot, so sloppy and young of him despite having finished the albino buck with it.

He had a dozen questions he wanted to put forth to Eva but not a single inclination to visit the witch. It'd only taken a single mention.

"Old Man, if it's all the same to you, I'd rather not hear the woman's name," C.V. had said.

Yet Fisher had also noticed his freezer was one frozen milk jug of fish lighter, of that he was certain, and he decided it best to let it sit with C.V. Deal a while.

Sunlight teased itself through the ice crystals of the cirrus clouds, and a couple of sundogs emerged as late afternoon drew on around Old Man Fisher. He paused to rest a little while under the coverts of the flaring, ancient limbs of the live oak on the edge of the field. There had been plenty of acorns this year, and it would be plenty cold this winter. His stump told him so, and he figured what was left of that albino buck wasn't going anywhere anytime soon, no matter how magnificent that spread on its rack, waiting to be tacked under eaves of the faring pens.

Down at the tangle of fence and the albino buck's carcass, a lone black dog eased out, hunched down, and threw back its head. Whether its eerie soft baying or the breeze moaning over the field, Fisher couldn't tell. A crow swooped down and hectored the *cusith*, snapping impotently and jumping.

Crow and black dog vanished back into the treeline. There came a song and laughter shadowing Old Man Fisher's trudge back to the trailer along with his tumbling thoughts.

Just maybe he'd have a visitor and not have to drink alone.

> *"Ci fenist le roumans*
> *De Perceval le Galois*
> *Lequel fu moult preus et courtois*
> *Et plain de grant chevalerie"*

> —*Le Conte Du Graal*

AFTERWORD

THE STORY YOU JUST READ SPUN ITSELF FROM SEVERAL SKEINS of yarn, so to speak. I've always loved hunting and fishing stories. Throw a rock in any direction here in the Deep South, and you're liable to hit someone recounting one or the other with enthusiasm, gravitas, and not a little embellishment. The quests and chases of Arthurian romance lend themselves to handy dovetailing with the aforementioned tales. Stumbling one day on a brief mention of the white stag legend from the Second Continuation of *Perceval* morphed into the framework for what I hoped to explore in having a go at the Fisher King and Perceval, Old Man Fisher and C.V. Deal respectively. Speaking of Continuations, it's refreshing to know Arthuriana is alive and well, able to grow with subsequent retellings much like a good fishing story. Between the fishing our noble and doughty, if maimed, king loved doing and the whole coursing-the-white-stag bit of the Second Continuation, I had my jumping off point for "Folk Unstuck..."

In "A Matter of Anachronisms,..." there's hint enough of the caregiving nature of C.V. Deal and the aged (and ailing) Old Man Fisher. For all of C.V.'s smart aleck nature and constant borrowing, never returning, the surrogacy evident in his and Fisher's relationship brings out, I hope, the best in C.V. Deal. "Folk Unstuck..." allowed more room to stretch the legs of that interplay while painting a few deeper brushstrokes on Fisher himself along with Eva.

Speaking of, across two stories, I never thought she'd be the one who was really the most fun to write. There she is, living on the fringes of the Penderton family's property. She is cryptic and frustrating and playful, if not a touch aloof and maternal. Of these various old souls, she's the most self-aware, and if she comes across as indiscriminate as nature itself, well, then she is a nature goddess at her core. She's a ready stand-in until I get to another story where Merlin finally comes into play, but Woman as Nurturer suits her just fine for Art while a touch of Temptress works for Old Man Fisher and, perhaps, C.V. Deal. But she's good to have around in a pinch despite all that.

Those creatures parlous strange in the *cusith*, quite frankly, make my skin crawl. I've been fascinated for years by the legends and contemporary anecdotes surrounding the black dogs and their various iterations. One does not deal lightly with the harbingers of doom. There's a part of me thinking one person's ghosts are another's black dogs (or demons or skeletons in closets—choose from the menu of handy metaphors), and the way the highways and dirt roads and trails wind down here, you can bet there's something on something else's trail. Or somebody's.

Memories. Ghosts. Dreams. Nightmares.

Just all black dogs, actually, laying in wait for a white stag and maybe even the one you're chasing.

—BCH

ACKNOWLEDGEMENTS

The roughing occurs in relative isolation, but the polishing needs getting by with a little (or more than a little) help from friends.

For the support and encouragement from the outset several years ago: Paul Jessup and Darin Bradley. You guys welcomed this Southern magical realism stuff with open arms.

For feedback, general and specific, along with not a few marks from the Red Pen of Doom: Michael Johnson, Peter M. Bush, Clint Harris (Red Pen of Doom #1), and Bill Preston (Red Pen of Doom #2).

To Murph: Even though it's fantasy, and there are monsters, my guys have guns. Right?

To Brad: Thank you for calling a spade a spade at times. And for coffee and critiquing.

To the LiveJournal friends-list: Thank you for dropping by when snippets were posted here and there. Your time and comments meant much. Still do.

To my editor: Erzebet, I appreciate how you have spoiled me the past few years by welcoming these pieces and helping me reach an audience as well as including me in so much of the process.

CPSIA information can be obtained at www.ICGtesting.com
Printed in the USA
LVOW02s1614291113

363018LV00010BA/61/P